Dear Dragon Goes to the Zoo

by Margaret Hillert

Illustrated by David Schimmell

NORWOOD HOUSE PRESS

DEAR CAREGIVER,

The *Beginning-to-Read* series is a carefully written collection of classic readers you may remember from your own childhood. Each book features text comprised of common sight words to provide your child ample practice reading the words that appear most frequently in written text. The many additional details in the pictures enhance the story and offer the opportunity for you to help your child expand oral language and develop comprehension.

Begin by reading the story to your child, followed by letting him or her read familiar words and soon your child will be able to read the story independently. At each step of the way, be sure to praise your reader's efforts to build his or her confidence as an independent reader. Discuss the pictures and encourage your child to make connections between the story and his or her own life. At the end of the story, you will find reading activities and a word list that will help your child practice and strengthen beginning reading skills.

Above all, the most important part of the reading experience is to have fun and enjoy it!

Shannon Cannon

Shannon Cannon,
Literacy Consultant

To Jim and Marie—
Good neighbors and zoo devotees. —M.H.

Norwood House Press • P.O. Box 316598 • Chicago, Illinois 60631
For more information about Norwood House Press please visit our website at
www.norwoodhousepress.com or call 866-565-2900.

LIBRARY OF CONGRESS CATALOGING-IN-PUBLICATION DATA
Hillert, Margaret.
   Dear dragon goes to the zoo / by Margaret Hillert ; illustrated by David Schimmell.
     p. cm. -- (A beginning-to-read book)
   Summary: "A boy and his pet dragon visit the zoo and see animals of all
different shapes and sizes"--Provided by publisher.
   ISBN-13: 978-1-59953-348-3 (library edition : alk. paper)
   ISBN-10: 1-59953-348-0 (library edition : alk. paper)
[1. Dragons--Fiction. 2. Zoos--Fiction.] I. Schimmell, David, ill. II. Title. PZ7.H558Del 2010
   [E]--dc22
                                   2009031727
Manufactured in the United States of America in North Mankato, Minnesota. 160N—072010

This looks like a good day,
a good day to go somewhere.
Do you want to go to the zoo?

The zoo?
Oh, yes Mother.
That will be fun!

Put this on—
and this—
and get into the car.

Here we go.
Away, away, away.

Here we are at the zoo.
You will like this.

ZOO

R1972M

Now we will walk and see things.
Look there!

This is a big one!
And so is the baby.

Oh, oh, oh.
What big cats!
See them run.

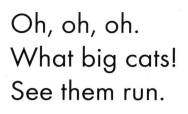

Look up there!
Way up, up, UP!

Oh, what a pretty one!
I like that one.

Look here.
The bears have a ball to play with.
A big red ball.

Oh, Father.
Look at this.
It is so big, big, BIG.

Oh, oh, oh.
And look here.
They like to jump!

Petting Zoo

Mother, look at this brown cow.
It is big.
Big, big, big.

Here is a pretty pony.
It would be fun to ride.

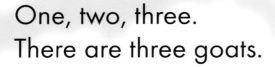

One, two, three.
There are three goats.

And two white bunnies.

This is pretty.
We can eat here.
Come and eat.

This is good, Mother.
This is a good spot.

Here you are with me.
And here I am with you.
What a good, good day, dear dragon.

The following activities support the findings of the National Reading Panel that determined the most effective components for reading instruction are: Phonemic Awareness, Phonics, Vocabulary, Fluency, and Text Comprehension.

Phonemic Awareness: The /z/ sound

1. Say the words **zoo**, **wizard**, and **buzz** and ask your child to repeat the /**z**/ sound after each.

2. Explain to your child that you are going to say some words and you would like her/him to show you one finger if the /**z**/ sound in the word is at the beginning, as in **zoo**; two fingers if the /**z**/ sound in the word is in the middle, as in **wizard**; or three fingers if the /**z**/ sound in the word is at the end, as in **buzz**.

zero (1)	dozen (2)	prize (3)	zipper (1)	buzzard (2)
girls (3)	daisy (2)	quiz (3)	cars (3)	easy (2)
zone (1)	roses (2&3)			

Phonics: The letters z and s

1. Demonstrate how to form the letters **z** and **s** for your child. Have your child practice writing **z** and **s** at least three times each.

2. Explain to your child that sometimes the **s** sounds like /**z**/.

3. Divide a piece of paper in half by folding it the long way. Draw a line on the fold. Turn it so that the paper has two columns. Write the letters **z** and **s** at the top of the columns.

4. Write the words from the list above on separate index cards. Ask your child to place the words in the correct column based on how the /**z**/ sound is spelled (with a **z** or **s**).

Word Work: ABC Order

1. Ask your child to recite the alphabet. Write the letters of the alphabet on a piece of paper and sing the alphabet song together while pointing at the letters as you go.

2. Write the following words on separate index cards: and, at, away, baby, big, can, cat, day, dear, dragon, eat, fun, get, good, here, is, it, jump, like, now, play, put, the, them, there, they, up, way, with, yes, zoo.

3. Place the words **and, big, can** (mix up the order) in front of your child. Ask your child to name the first letter in each word.

4. Tell your child that you are going to work together to put the words in alphabetical order by looking at the first letter in each word. Help your child put the words in order.

5. Next, put the words **the, them, they** (mix up the order) in front of your child.

6. Tell your child that when words begin with the same letter, we put them in order based on the next letters. Help your child put the words in alphabetical order (using the fourth letter).

7. Now work with your child to put the remaining words in alphabetical order.

Fluency: Shared Reading/CLOZE

1. Reread the story with your child at least two more times while your child tracks the print by running a finger under the words as they are read. Ask your child to read the words he or she knows with you.

2. Reread the story, stopping occasionally so your child can supply the next word. For example, *It looks like a good* _____ (day), or *The bears have a* _____ (ball) *to play with*, or *Here is a pretty* _____ (pony).

3. Now have your child reread the story, stopping occasionally for you to supply the next word.

Text Comprehension: Discussion Time

1. Ask your child to retell the sequence of events in the story.

2. To check comprehension, ask your child the following questions:
   • Which animals could the boy get close to and pet?
   • What did the monkeys like to do?
   • What is your favorite animal in the zoo? Why?

WORD LIST

Dear Dragon Goes to the Zoo **uses the 78 words listed below.**
This list can be used to practice reading the words that appear in the text.
You may wish to write the words on index cards and use them to help your
child build automatic word recognition. Regular practice with these words
will enhance your child's fluency in reading connected text.

a	day	is	put	two
am	dear	it		
and	do		red	up
are	dragon	jump	ride	
at			run	walk
away	eat	like		want
		look(s)	see	way
baby	Father		so	we
ball	fun	me	somewhere	what
be		Mother	spot	white
bears	get			will
big	go	now	that	with
brown	goats		the	would
bunnies	good	oh	them	
		on	there	yes
can	have	one	they	you
car	here		things	
cats		play	this	zoo
come	I	pony	three	
cow	into	pretty	to	

Photograph by Glenna Washburn

ABOUT THE AUTHOR Margaret Hillert has written over 80 books for
children who are just learning to read. Her books
have been translated into many different languages and over a million children
throughout the world have read her books. She first started writing poetry as
a child and has continued to write for children and adults throughout her life. A
first grade teacher for 34 years, Margaret is now retired from teaching and lives in
Michigan where she likes to write, take walks in the morning, and care for her three cats.

ABOUT THE ADVISER Shannon Cannon contributed the activities pages that appear in
this book. Shannon serves as a literacy consultant and provides
staff development to help improve reading instruction. She is a frequent presenter at educational
conferences and workshops. Prior to this she worked as an elementary school teacher and as
president of a curriculum publishing company.